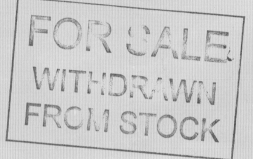

This Little Tiger Book Belongs To:

_____

_____

_____

_____

For Annie
~A.M.

For the Farmhouse Mice
~T.W.

LITTLE TIGER PRESS
An imprint of Magi Publications
1 The Coda Centre
189 Munster Road, London SW6 6AW
www.littletigerpress.com
This paperback edition published in 2002
First published in Great Britain 2002
Text © 2002 Alan MacDonald
Illustrations © 2002 Tim Warnes
Alan MacDonald and Tim Warnes have
asserted their rights to be identified as the
hor and illustrator of this work under the
opyright, Designs and Patents Act, 1988.
Printed in Belgium

SCAREDY MOUSE

Alan
MACDONALD

★ ★ ★

Tim
WARNES

LITTLE TIGER PRESS

London

In a small hole behind a
cupboard under the stairs lived
a large family of mice.
The youngest was called Squeak.
Squeak was a small mouse,
a scared mouse,
a stay-at-home mouse.

Squeak!

One evening, Squeak was woken up
by his sister, Nibbles.
"Let's go to the kitchen," she said.
"I've just seen something yummy.
A chocolate cake as big as a wheel."

Squeak loved chocolate, but he was very scared.
"What if I get lost?" he worried.
"What if we meet the big ginger cat with green eyes?"
"The ginger cat's asleep," said Nibbles. "And I know how to stop you getting lost."

Nibbles fetched a big ball of string,
and tied one end round Squeak.
"There," she said. "All you have to
do is to follow the string and you'll
find your way home."

They scurried out of the mousehole,
and into the dark, shadowy hall.
Squeak kept close to Nibbles, trailing
the string behind him. But as they crossed
the hall, Squeak saw a long, stripy tail.

"IT'S THE CAT, IT'S THE CAT!"
he cried.
Squeak ran this way and that,
harum-scarum, round and back.
"Don't be silly," said Nibbles . . .

Squeak slowly came out of his hiding place.

Through the dining room scampered
Nibbles and Squeak. Under the table and
under the chairs. But just as Squeak was
about to eat a biscuit crumb, he saw two
eyes gleaming in the dark.

"IT'S THE CAT, IT'S THE CAT!"
he cried.
Squeak ran this way and that,
harum-scarum, round and back.
"Don't be silly," said Nibbles . . .

Squeak smiled nervously.

Into the lounge they stole, past the
fireplace, and past the ticking clock.
Suddenly, Squeak froze in his tracks.
There, peeping above the arm of the
chair, was a head with two sharp ears.

"IT'S THE CAT, IT'S THE CAT!"
he cried.
Squeak ran this way and that,
harum-scarum, round and back.
"Don't be silly," said Nibbles . . .

"Silly me!" said Squeak.

Into the kitchen tiptoed the two mice, across the floorboards and past the cupboard. Squeak peeped inside.
He shivered and shook.
There, in the shadows, was something furry.

"*IT'S THE CAT,
IT'S THE CAT!*"
he cried.
Squeak ran this way
and that, harum-scarum,
round and back.
"Don't be silly," said
Nibbles . . .

"Phew!" sighed Squeak.

Just then, Nibbles spotted the chocolate cake
on the fridge. It didn't take them long to find
their way up to it. Soon their paws and whiskers
were licky and sticky with chocolate.

"Yum," sighed Nibbles. "I could eat all day."
Squeak was a hungry mouse,
but also a worried mouse,
a scared mouse,
a want-to-go-home mouse.

So Nibbles scrambled down the fridge . . .

and Squeak and the cake followed.

They heaved the cake across the floor, but . . .

just as they reached the door,
a shadow fell across their path.
"*IT'S THE CAT, IT'S THE CAT!*"
cried Squeak.
"Don't be silly," said Nibbles.
"It's only . . .

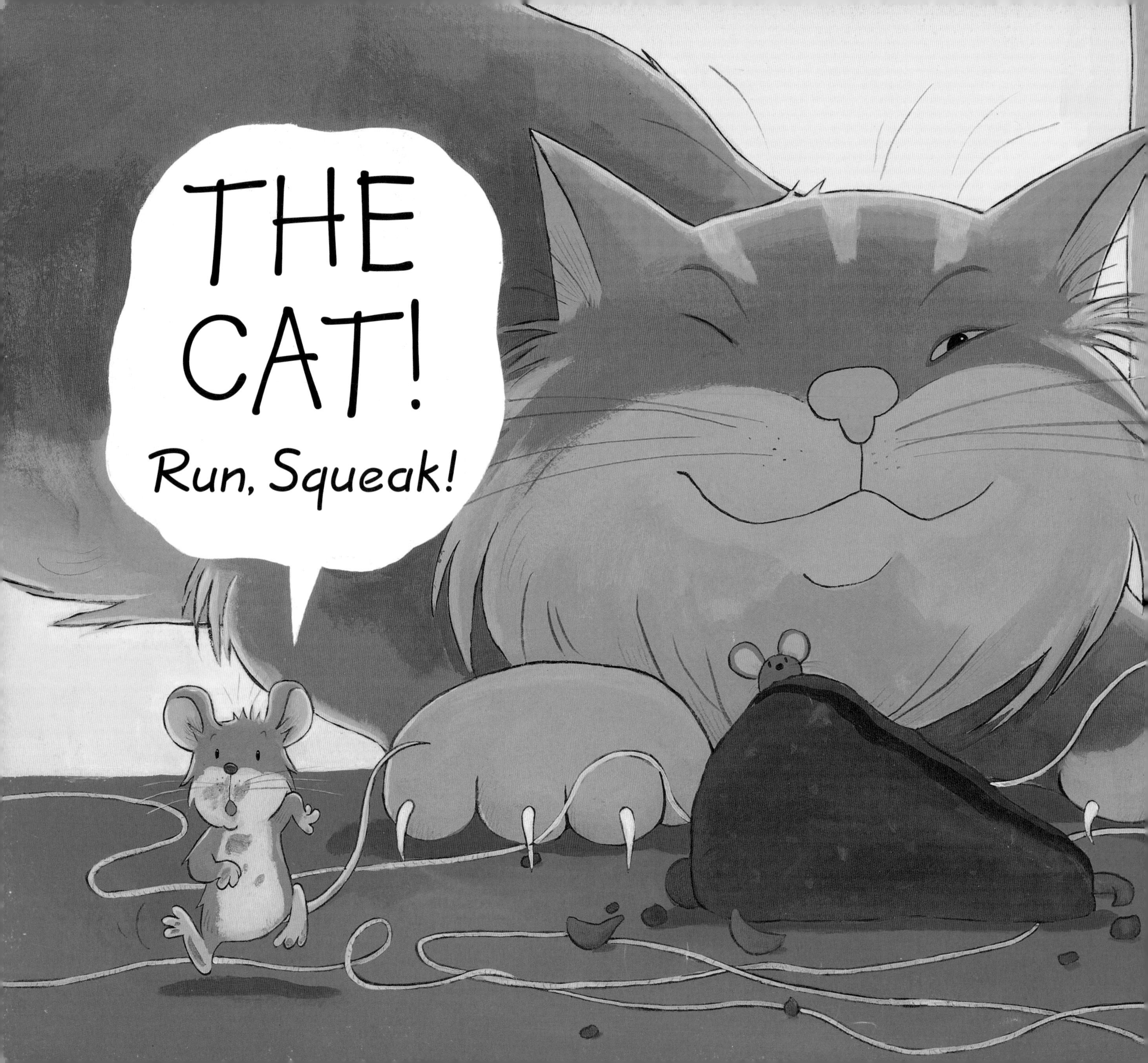
THE CAT!
Run, Squeak!

Squeak ran this way and that,
harum-scarum, round and back.
The big ginger cat narrowed his eyes,
opened his claws and . . .

EEEK!

pounced.
But the cat found himself caught in a
web of string. The more he struggled,
the more he became tangled . . .

until soon he was tied up
like a fat ginger parcel.
A mad cat,
a sad cat,
a feeling-a-fool cat.

Squeak was no longer a small or a scared mouse.
He was a bold-as-a-lion mouse.

And the next time he met the
big ginger cat, he just said . . .

OTHER COLOURFUL STORIES FROM LITTLE TIGER PRESS

For information regarding any of the above titles or for our catalogue, please contact us:
Little Tiger Press, 1 The Coda Centre, 189 Munster Road, London SW6 6AW, UK.
Telephone: 020 7385 6333 Fax: 020 7385 7333 e-mail: info@littletiger.co.uk
www.littletigerpress.com